Scaredy Bat
and the Frozen Vampires

By Marina J. Bowman

Illustrated by Yevheniia Lisovaya

Code Pineapple

First paperback edition September 2019

Written by Marina J. Bowman
Illustrated by Yevheniia Lisovaya
Book design by Tobi Carter
Cover design by Vanessa Mendozzi

ISBN 978-1-950341-06-1 (paperback color)
ISBN 978-1-950341-07-8 (paperback black & white)
ISBN 978-1-950341-08-5 (ebook)

Published by Code Pineapple
www.codepineapple.com

For all of you - vampire, human, or otherwise - that have been afraid of something, but didn't let that stop you.

Also by Marina J. Bowman

SCAREDY BAT

A supernatural detective series for kids with courage, teamwork, and problem solving. If you like solving mysteries and overcoming fears, you'll love this enchanting tale!

#1 Scaredy Bat and the Frozen Vampires

#2 Scaredy Bat and the Sunscreen Snatcher

#3 Scaredy Bat and the Missing Jellyfish

THE LEGEND OF PINEAPPLE COVE

A fantasy-adventure series for kids with bravery, kindness, and friendship. If you like reimagined mythology and animal sidekicks, you'll love this legendary story!

#1 Poseidon's Storm Blaster

#2 A Mermaid's Promise

#3 King of the Sea

#4 Protector's Pledge

Do you have what it takes to be a detective?

Take the FREE
Detective Skills Assessment
to find out!

GO HERE TO GET
YOUR ASSESSMENT NOW:

scaredybat.com/book1bonus

Detective Team

Jessica
"the courage"

Ellie
aka Scaredy Bat
"the detective"

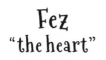

Fez
"the heart"

Tink
"the brains"

Contents

Batty Bonuses

Can you solve the mystery?

All you need is an eye for detail, a sharp memory, and good logical skills. Join Ellie on her mystery-solving adventure by making a suspect list and figuring out who committed the crime! To help with your sleuthing, you'll find a suspect list template and hidden details observation sheets at the back of the book.

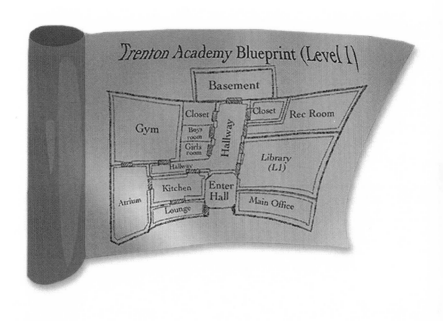

There's a place not far from here
With strange things 'round each corner
It's a town where vampires walk the streets
And unlikely friendships bloom

When there's a mystery to solve
Ellie Spark is the vampire to call
Unless she's scared away like a cat
Poof! There goes that Scaredy Bat

Villains and pesky sisters beware
No spider, clown, or loud noise
Will stop Ellie and her team
From solving crime, one fear at a time

Chapter One
Poof!

Ellie stomped down the hall to her little sister's room only to find pesky Penny nowhere in sight. "Penny!" Ellie cried. "Did you steal my favorite purple dragon necklace?" Ellie dug through the toybox and the closet before laying eyes on Penny's pink coffin bed. She whipped up the sheet to peek underneath, but what she found definitely wasn't her necklace.

Her breath caught in the back of her throat. A hairy spider the size of a watermelon sat just behind the sheet, all eight of his eyes hungrily glaring at Ellie.

"AIYEE!" Ellie shrieked. *POOF!* Just like that she transformed into a bat and flapped into the closet.

"Ha-ha! Got you!" a voice boasted from under the bed. A small girl with straight brown hair and green eyes, much like Ellie's, crawled out from under the coffin bed.

"That's not funny!" Ellie squeaked as she flew out of the closet and transformed back into a vampire. *POOF!*

A large smile spread across Penny's face. "I think it is! It's not my fault you're a big Scaredy Bat. Scaredy Bat! Scaredy Bat! Ellie is a Scaredy Bat!"

Ellie's face grew hot with embarrassment and anger. "Listen, you little brat, when I get my hands on you..." Ellie lunged for her sister, throwing them both onto the pink coffin, where Ellie promptly cocooned Penny in the purple bed sheets before smacking her with a sparkly throw pillow.

"Mom! MOM!" Penny cried.

A woman with curled black hair and a blood-red dress appeared in the bedroom doorway. "What is going on here?" demanded Mom. "Ellie, leave Penny alone!"

Ellie hesitantly backed away from her sister, but not before giving her one more good thwack with the pillow.

Mom stepped up beside Ellie and snatched the pillow. "What is going on?" she asked again.

"She started it!" the two sisters bellowed in unison. Ellie continued, "Penny scared me with… with… THAT." She pointed to the large spider sitting on the floor.

"I just wanted to play! It's not my fault you're scared of everything," sneered Penny.

"It was a giant spider and spiders are gross. How could I not be scared?" Ellie countered.

Suddenly, a purple glimmer in the corner of the room caught Ellie's eye. She whipped her head around to see her sister's favorite bear, Miss Batty. She was wearing the purple necklace!

Ellie raced over and lifted the necklace off the bear. "Another mystery solved by The Great Vampire Detective!" She held up the necklace like an Olympic medal.

Penny snorted. "You have to solve *real* mysteries to be a detective."

Ellie lurched forward for another pillow, but Mom scooped it up before she could get there.

"Okay, that's enough," Mom snapped. "Ellie, you need to finish getting ready or we will be late."

"Why can't I go?" whined Penny, tears pooling in her large eyes.

Mom sighed. "We've already talked about this. No one under twelve can attend the wedding, but don't worry, you'll have a lot more fun with Grandma at the pool today. After all, it is the hottest day of the year."

"Why does Ellie get to go?"

"Because I'm twelve now," Ellie said, beaming. "So, ha!"

"We're lucky that any of us get to go to such an important event," Mom explained. "If your father hadn't performed emergency surgery on King Stanton last year, we wouldn't even be invited."

Before Ellie or Penny could reply, a short

and stout woman with a mixing bowl appeared beside Mom. She looked at Penny, who was still tangled in blankets. "Come on, my Little Fang. I made a batch of fresh blood pudding!"

Penny's eyes grew wide with excitement. "Okay, Grandma!"

Thoughts of the wedding quickly fled and Ellie's mouth watered as she thought about her favorite treat. She loved blood pudding, especially Grandma's since she always made it the best way—extra bloody. "Can I have some pudding, too?" Ellie asked.

Grandma smiled. "Oh, dear, I think you have to go, but I'm sure Penny will save you some."

"No, I won't," Penny proclaimed as she freed herself from the last of the bed sheets. She followed Grandma out into the hall, but not before sticking her tongue out at Ellie.

"Mom, she stuck her tongue out at me!" Ellie complained, prompting Penny to run downstairs.

Mrs. Spark didn't seem to hear her oldest daughter. She fiddled with her wedding rings,

something Ellie knew she only did when she was nervous.

She finally looked over at Ellie. "Did you say something?"

Ellie lied and shook her head.

"Ellie, I need you to be on your best behaviour today. This wedding is very important."

"It's just a fancy wedding," Ellie said.

Mom shook her head. "No, no, it is not. Prince Bennett's brother, Theo, dug up some ancient royal rule yesterday evening, and it turns out that if Bennett doesn't get married by seven o'clock tonight, then the crown falls to Theo. And if Theo gets the crown..." Mom paused as she looked down at her wedding rings. "He will reverse the Fang and Flesh Peace Treaty."

"What does that mean?" Ellie asked.

"That means that any state in the U.S. could choose to make vampire residents illegal again, humans and vampires couldn't get married anymore, and any vampires and humans currently married would be forced to separate."

A lump settled in Ellie's throat, like she

swallowed a golf ball. "You and Dad would have to separate?" Tears stung her eyes as she thought of her vampire Mom and human Dad forced to live apart.

Mom nodded, and her voice softened. "But you don't need to worry about that, love. The wedding is going to be just fine. That is, if we ever get there. Can we go now, please?"

Ellie made her way downstairs as thoughts of her parents separating swirled around her mind. Who would she live with? Would she and Penny live with the same parent? Penny drove her nuts, but she knew she would miss her pesky sister if she didn't get to see her all the time.

As if on cue, Penny excitedly popped in front of Ellie with more blood pudding on her face than in the flowered bowl she held. "Mmm!" she said in an extra loud voice. "This sure is good! Too bad you don't get any."

Okay, maybe Ellie wouldn't miss Penny that much.

"Ellie! Dad is waiting for us in the car. We need to go!" Mom called from across the

house. Ellie rushed out the door, but not before grabbing her favorite turquoise detective coat. She always kept Monster Spray in the pocket, just in case.

Chapter Two
Trenton Academy

The Jotun Frost Giants have made it clear that they favor the end of the Fang and Flesh Peace Treaty and would welcome a vampire king like Prince Theo. This is what their leader had to say—" The sound of the car's radio was replaced by chirping birds as Ellie stepped out of the blue car. The scent of flowers wafted through the air. Ellie and her parents walked up to a towering metal gate that surrounded a large building. With its sun-washed bricks, high arched windows, and glass atrium, the former paper mill's mix of vintage charm and modern beauty was like many of the buildings in Brookside. What was once a remote ghost town in the northern

U.S. known for its failed paper mill was now a thriving community with lush forests, a famous garlic festival, and of course, Trenton Academy.

Trenton Academy was the first school to allow both vampire and human students—even before the Fang and Flesh Peace Treaty—and now it was the chosen venue for the Royal Vampire Wedding.

"*This* is where the Royal Vampire Wedding is?" Ellie asked as she scrunched her nose. "Why would anyone want to have their wedding at a stinky middle school?" While stunning to most with its historical elegance and colorful garden beds, all Ellie could see was a place with mandatory Monday math quizzes and cafeteria food that resembled grey mush.

Dad looked at the secret location that was sent to his phone a mere hour ago. "Yup, this is definitely it."

Mom nudged Ellie and flashed her daughter a look that Ellie knew meant 'behave.' "I'm sure it will be beautiful."

"But why would you get married here when you have a dream palace in the forest?" asked Ellie.

"They wanted it to be a bit more private," answered Dad. "Plus, this school is kind of fitting, since Ayanna is the first human to be married into the Royal Vampire family. Don't you think?"

"I guess," mumbled Ellie. A man in a black suit and a woman in a pink poufy dress distracted Ellie from her disapproval of the venue choice. They stood in the school's attached atrium, holding a piece of paper and small flashlight. *Why do they need a flashlight to read in clear daylight?* Ellie wondered. As the man read to the woman in pink, Ellie tried to read his lips—a detective skill she never seemed to master—while Mom inserted a gold key card into a monitor on the gate.

"GREETINGS!" boomed a robotic voice.

Ellie jumped at the overly loud welcome. "Please standby for a face scan." As a red laser skipped across the trio's faces, Ellie looked back at the atrium, but the couple had disappeared. After a few seconds the voice sounded once

more. "Thank you, Gina Spark, Dr. Harold Spark, and Ellie Spark. You may enter."

Ellie stood with her mouth open as the gate creaked forward. This may be her familiar middle school, but that was definitely new. It was just like a cool piece of tech that her idol, Hailey Haddie, would encounter in her favorite mystery series, *The Amazing Vampire Detective*. She couldn't wait to see what else was inside.

Ellie's amazement grew as they entered the school gym. It no longer looked like the place where smelly boys spilled sweat on the basketball court and gym teachers yelled at her to run faster. Her eyes gleamed as she took in the bright flowers around every corner and elegant ice sculptures in each room. White flowing fabric and twinkle lights hung from the ceiling like sparkly clouds. It looked like a wedding from a fairy tale.

"You made it!" cried a familiar voice behind Ellie.

Ellie turned around to the familiarity of red curls and a bright white, fanged smile. "Jessica!" Ellie gushed. The two girls hugged as if

they hadn't seen each other in weeks, when in reality it had only been a couple days.

"Can you believe this used to be the gym? It looks amazing!" gushed Jessica.

Ellie nodded as she took in more of the stunning decor.

Jessica pointed to a rather poised woman with a light blue dress that perfectly contrasted her tan skin. "That's Shayla Jeffords, the wedding planner," Jessica explained. "My mom said that if she ever gets married again, she would definitely hire Shayla."

Ellie's eyes wandered to Jessica's mom, Camille Perry. Her hair was straight and sleek, unlike her daughter's mess of curls, but those gray-blue eyes were undoubtedly one of the traits that the mother and daughter duo shared, along with their effortless charm that seemed to make everyone like them. Ellie supposed that if you were going to be a big-time actress like Camille Perry, that charm was a must. Ellie refocused on Jessica, who was still chattering on about the wedding.

"…And I hear that some of the food has been specially catered so that it has *never* been tasted before this wedding. Although, I hear they have some frozen desserts, and I don't know how anything will stay frozen for more than a second on the hottest day of the year." Jessica finally caught a breath as she wiped a small bead of sweat from her brow.

"It is super hot today," Ellie said as she tugged at her jacket's collar.

Jessica nodded. "I know. I am so warm. How are you not boiling in that turquoise trench coat?"

Ellie looked down at her long coat. She loved it, but maybe Jessica had a point. She stripped off the jacket, revealing her pink dress and purple stockings with crescent moons. Ellie noted that it wasn't nearly as elegant as Jessica's dark blue dress with subtle sparkles, but she still stood by her choice.

Jessica looked at a nearby air vent and fanned herself with her hand. "Do you want to go outside for a bit?" she asked. "They said they won't start the wedding until the air conditioning kicks in more, so we have a little while."

Ellie nodded. "Sure! Just let me ask my parents." The gym may look nice, but it still felt like the same hot and sticky school Ellie remembered. After her parents agreed, the two girls made their way to the front door just as a short boy in a tux with dark skin and glasses rushed past them.

"Hey, isn't that the boy that had the project that caught last year's science fair on fire?" Ellie whispered.

"I think so," replied Jessica. "On the bright side, it ruined our project, so we automatically got an A."

"That's right!" said Ellie. Both girls laughed.

With the front doors locked, the attached atrium was the closest they could get to outside. It was a quiet space with windowed walls, colorful flowers, and lush greenery. After Ellie and Jessica gushed over the wedding and Ellie complained about her latest fight with Penny, the two friends decided it was time to go back in. As Ellie stood, she plucked a dandelion that was invading one of the pots and blew on the willowy, white seeds. *I wish I could solve a real mystery*, she thought to herself. Just then, she looked up to see Jessica tugging on the glass door, which was sheeted with a sudden, mysterious layer of frost.

Chapter Three
What Do We Know

T he door won't budge!" Jessica exclaimed.

"I think it might be frozen shut," Ellie said, pointing to the ice on the other side of the glass.

With a few more tugs from the duo, the door snapped open and a refreshing cold breeze wisped through the atrium.

"I guess the air conditioning is working now," said Ellie.

"Must be," Jessica agreed.

A piece of paper fluttered down and landed by Ellie's feet.

"What's that?" Jessica asked.

Ellie picked up the sheet, flipped it over a few times, and shrugged. "It's blank."

"Keep it for later!" Jessica insisted. "That way if the wedding is boring, we can pass notes, like we do in class."

Ellie looked down at her pocketless dress and decided to tuck the paper into her shoe.

As the two made their way to the gym, the refreshing breeze soon turned to an aggressive wash of cold that sent both Jessica and Ellie into a shiver frenzy. They peeked through the propped open gym door to find that not only had the air conditioning kicked in, the vents now blew chunky snowflakes throughout the frozen room.

"What happened!?" Jessica shrieked.

Ellie looked at the thick layer of ice that covered almost every surface, including all the guests, who were now frozen statues. Both girls shivered as they took in the snowy scene. "I guess the air conditioning *really* decided to work," Ellie said wearily. Then it dawned on her. "Where are my parents?" Ellie rushed in and found her mom in the back corner—frozen mid-laughter with a wine glass in her hand— while her father stood not much farther with a smile bending up both corners of his lips.

Jessica stood beside her own mother. "Mom. MOM! Can you hear me?" she shouted, but there was no answer.

"We need to call the police," Ellie said.

Jessica nodded. She snapped open her mom's bag and pulled out a small silver phone. She poked at the screen as her teeth began to

chatter. "It's too cold; the touchscreen isn't working. We need to go back to the atrium."

Ellie rubbed her arms. Jessica was right; they couldn't stay here much longer. "I'll get you out of there soon," Ellie whispered to her parents. The two girls raced back to the welcoming warmth of the atrium.

"Here, y-you try d-dialing?" stammered Jessica, still trying to shake off the cold.

Ellie grabbed the phone, and after a few tries, she successfully dialed 9-1-1.

"911, what's your emergency?"

"Everyone is frozen!" Ellie exclaimed.

"Okay, miss. I am going to need more details."

"My friend Jessica and I went inside the atrium at the Royal Vampire Wedding, and when we came back, the whole gym was frozen solid!"

"And where are you?" asked the operator.

"Trenton Academy."

"So, you're at a middle school, which is hosting the royal wedding, and everyone is suddenly frozen on the hottest day of the year?"

"Yes!" confirmed Ellie.

The operator laughed. "Wow, you have one imagination, kid. I'm sorry, but I have to keep this line open for real emergencies, but thanks for giving me a good chuckle." The call ended.

Ellie's mouth gaped in disbelief. "They didn't believe me!"

"What!?" cried Jessica. "But it's true! What do we do now?"

Ellie's stomach did a somersault as she spotted the wish flower that she'd blown on only minutes ago, wishing for a real mystery. A wave of guilt washed over her as she thought about her parents and the ruined wedding's consequences, for them and the rest of the world. She took a deep breath before finally answering, "I think we have to fix this ourselves."

Ellie explained the urgency of the wedding and the consequences if Prince Theo came into power and abolished the Fang and Flesh Peace Treaty.

"That's horrible!" exclaimed Jessica. "So, what should we do first?"

"Well, what do we know? It was super cold in there, almost like a blizzard."

"Which seems nearly impossible on such a hot day," Jessica added as thoughts of the cold gym sent a shiver down her spine.

"And the freezing happened fast. We were just in there and it was still pretty warm, plus everyone that's frozen looks like they were having a good time," Ellie deducted.

"Right." Jessica nodded. "So, what or who could have made that happen?"

"Prince Theo wants the crown, so maybe he did this?"

"But how? It went from boiling to freezing so fast," Jessica said.

"Let's look for clues," suggested Ellie.

Jessica shivered. "Okay, but can we maybe check in here first? I'm still cold."

"Sure," Ellie agreed.

The two girls split up and searched the large atrium. Instantly, Ellie noticed that the atrium's fountain wasn't frozen. So why was the rest of the school so cold? Her eyes wandered to the

glass ceiling as a large boot-shaped cloud blew into view.

"Oh my gosh, of course!" Ellie squealed.

"What?" Jessica asked eagerly.

"A Jotun Frost Giant did this," Ellie replied.

Jessica's eyes grew wide. "A what?"

"Yeah, a what?" came a voice from behind them.

Chapter Four
Rock, Bat, Dagger

The two girls jumped, and *POOF!*, Ellie transformed into a bat and darted into a nearby tree.

Beside a wooden bench stood a stocky boy in an apron licking a dripping ice cream cone. He looked at Ellie in the tree as trails of vanilla and chocolate made their way down his arm. "Wow, that's awesome!" he marveled.

"Who are you?" demanded Jessica.

POOF! "Yeah, what she said," added Ellie, now back in her vampire form.

The boy licked a run of ice cream that streamed down his arm. "Fizz," he said as he slurped up the last drip.

"Fizz?" questioned Ellie. "What kind of name is that?"

The boy laughed as he shoved the last of his cone into his mouth and wiped his hands on his apron. "Fez, not Fizz," he explained after he swallowed the last of his treat.

"Wait a second," said Jessica, "don't you go to our school?"

Fez nodded. "Yup, I recognize you two." He held out his hand. "It's nice to officially meet you!"

Jessica and Ellie both looked down at the boy's chubby fingers, still visibly covered in melted ice cream. Not wanting to be rude, they both accepted the sticky handshake and introduced themselves.

"My Dad is catering the wedding," Fez said. "I was helping him get the food ready in the cafeteria kitchen when suddenly a huge blast of cold air and snow shot through the school!"

"I knew it!" boasted Ellie. "I knew it had to have been sudden."

Jessica, however, didn't share in Ellie's excitement. "Hey Fez," said Jessica, "if you were inside

28

like you claim to be, then why didn't you freeze?"

Fez shrugged. "I was wondering that too, but I figure it must have been because I have so much of my dad's secret hot sauce on me. It gives off a ton of heat!"

Jessica and Ellie glanced at each other, both thinking it was an unlikely story.

"There is no way a sauce could give off that much heat," Ellie spat.

"See for yourself," insisted Fez. He handed a small bag of thick, red sauce to Ellie. It did feel warm, but how could it give off enough heat for someone not to be flash-frozen?

"It's not *that* hot," Ellie said matter-of-factly.

Fez snickered. "If you don't think it's hot, try some."

Ellie looked at Jessica. "Rock, Bat, Dagger to see who tries it?"

Jessica rolled her eyes and sighed. "Fine," she agreed.

The two girls stretched out their hands and chanted, "Rock, Bat, Dagger." Ellie's hand landed in the shape of a dagger and Jessica's in a rock-shaped fist.

"Ha! Rock beats dagger," Jessica said.

Ellie took a deep breath before squirting a large dollop onto her finger. "Well, here goes nothing," she gulped. She licked the warm goop off her finger and swished it around her mouth.

"Maybe you should have had a smaller taste," said Fez.

"Why?" asked Ellie. "This is—this is—oh my gosh! My mouth is on FIRE!" Ellie stuck out her tongue and panted like a dog.

Jessica looked over at Fez, who chuckled as Ellie ran around the atrium. "I'm going to say that your story checks out," chortled Jessica.

Fez's smile widened. "I'm glad, because it's the truth."

Ellie ran back over with her eyes watering and her tongue still hanging out. "That is the hottest thing I have ever tasted." She licked her lips. "It is quite tasty, though."

"Hey guys, earlier you said something about a Jelly Frost Giant? Is that some sort of snack? It sounds delicious!" said Fez.

Ellie laughed. "Jotun Frost Giant. They're
not a snack, they're these huge giants that live
in the mountains, but when they come out, they
create freakish blizzards and freeze things."

"That sure does sound like what happened
here." Jessica shuddered.

Fez gulped. "You think one did this?"

"When I was getting out of the car today, I heard on the radio that the Jotun Frost Giants would welcome a vampire king like Prince Theo. And they definitely have the power to freeze the school this fast."

Ellie looked around the atrium and raced to a corner under a bench. "Aha!" she exclaimed. "Proof that the Frost Giants were here."

Chapter Five
Shadow on the Horizon

E llie held up a grey ball of fluff. "Sometimes they ride giant wolves, and this definitely looks like wolf fur," she exclaimed.

Jessica and Fez ran over to get a better look at the clue. Jessica squinted as she examined the find. "You sure that's wolf fur?" she asked.

"It does kind of look like a big dust bunny," Fez said.

Ellie's proud smile quickly faded. "Well, I guess the wolf fur wouldn't be in here, since this part of the school isn't frozen. But maybe it blew in through the vents?"

The three looked around the room only to find no vents in sight.

Ellie dropped the grey dust bunny to the ground and wiped her hands on her dress. "There are really no cold mountains around here, though, and I doubt a Frost Giant would come all this way."

"Plus, I don't think they would risk angering the rest of the royal family," Jessica added.

Ellie's eyes grew wide. "But if Frost Giants didn't do this, what is that!" She pointed to a shadow on the horizon outside before *POOF!* She raced back into the nearby tree.

Fez and Jessica looked to where Ellie had pointed. "Ellie, all I see is a blue sky," Jessica said, perplexed.

"Me, too," agreed Fez.

POOF! Ellie popped back down from the tree and looked over at the spot where the giant's silhouette stood. "It's right there!" she cried.

Jessica looked at the spot and then over at Ellie. "Oh, Ellie." She laughed. She took Ellie's glasses off and wiped the lenses on her dress. "Here, now look again," Jessica said, handing Ellie her glasses.

Ellie put on her glasses, and felt her face grow hot. "Oh," she mumbled.

Fez chuckled. "So, Frost Giants are glasses smudges. Good to know."

Ellie put her hand on her hips. "No! Jotun Frost Giants live in cold, mountainous environments and can be super evil with their icy powers." She took her hands off her hips. "But I don't think they did this."

"What is sticking out of your shoe?" asked Fez.

Ellie pulled out the folded sheet. "Just a piece of blank paper we found in here earlier." Suddenly, she remembered the couple reading the paper in the atrium when she was at the gate. "We need to find the woman in a pink and poufy dress that I saw reading in the atrium with a man in a suit," she said. "I think this is written in invisible ink, so we need the special flashlight thing to read it, and she might have it."

"Oh, just like the jungle episode of *The Amazing Vampire Detective* where Hailey Haddie needs to send a secret note?" asked Fez.

"Exactly!" said Ellie.

Chapter Six

The Woman in Pink

Once again, they made their way into the frosty school. The biting cold nipped at every inch of them as they entered the gym. Ellie peeled her turquoise trench coat from where she left it and began searching for the pink dress. Everything was frozen. Even the photos of the royal couple had small icicles hanging from the frames. Ellie spotted a frozen woman wearing a puffy pink dress and a mean scowl on her face. What was she holding?

"Guys, I think I found her!" Ellie shouted.

Fez rushed over, and Ellie pointed to the woman.

"Hey, I recognize her," said Fez. "Earlier today I overheard her bragging about how

much better of a princess she would have made. Do you think she might be behind this?"

"Maybe she is jealous of Bennett marrying Ayanna and did this to ruin the wedding," offered Ellie. "But is that a wedding ring on her finger?"

"Yup," Jessica confirmed as she arrived. "She is married. My mom actually knows her. Her name is Talia, and she is Prince Bennett's ex-girlfriend. Although she is absolutely full of herself, I don't think she could have done this." She pointed to Talia's finger. "She's married, she's frozen, and not to sound mean, but I don't think she is clever enough."

Fez snickered. "Well, now that you mention it, she did mistake the kitchen area for the girl's washroom and repeatedly tried to pull open the door, even though it clearly says 'push'."

"Yup, that's definitely her," Jessica confirmed.

"But what about this?" Ellie said, pointing to the cylindrical, black item Talia held. She answered her own question, spotting a large moustache drawn on Ayanna's portrait.

"Are you going to bother giving someone a marker moustache if you plan to freeze their whole wedding?" Fez asked.

"Probably not," Ellie agreed. "I thought she was holding what we need to read the invisible ink."

"Her art does look pretty funny though," Jessica said, taking a few photos of the moustached photo with her mom's phone. As the biting cold intensified, the two girls could no longer fight off their shivers. "Let's check the lost-and-found for some warmer clothes," Jessica suggested.

Ellie tried to warm her hands with her breath. "That's a great idea!" she agreed.

The trio went to the nearby lost-and-found to find the bin that usually overflowed with mismatched mittens, scratchy scarves, and long forgotten coats nearly empty.

Fez reached in and picked up a frayed set of headphones, an oversized pink ruler, and a silver compact mirror. "Unless these can somehow keep a vampire warm, I don't think they will help."

Both girls huddled together as their shivering intensified. Ellie looked over at Fez searching through another bin in nothing but a t-shirt, apron, and shorts. How was he not cold?

Chapter Seven
The Man in the Photo

Aha!" Looking down at Fez's bulging pockets, Ellie found her answer. "Fez, do you have any extra hot sauce?" she asked.

"Is now really the time to think about your hunger?" Jessica snapped.

"No, Jess. Look how warm he is with that hot sauce in his pockets."

Jessica looked over at Fez. "Of course, that's why he's still warm. Just like how he avoided getting flash-frozen." Not only wasn't he shivering like Ellie and Jessica, but he even seemed to be sweating slightly.

Fez turned around to address Ellie's question. "Sure, there's lots in the kitchen. I'll be right back!" He bolted out of the room.

42

Jessica gave off a big shiver and looked over at Ellie. "Fez is really nice," she said. "When this is all over, we should definitely hang out with him."

"Definitely!" Ellie agreed. She looked up at the clock. *6:15.* They were running out of time.

"While we're waiting, I've been meaning to ask you. Do you want my yellow dress with the green flowers?" Jessica asked.

Although Ellie's mind was still in detective mode, she indulged her friend. "Which one is that again?"

"Hold on, I think my mom has a pic on her phone." Jessica opened the phone to the photo of the moustached Ayanna.

Who was that in the photo with her? Ellie thought. Jessica began to swipe past the photo. "Wait, go back!" Ellie said. Her eyes grew wide as she recognized that brown hair and face. "That's him! Prince Theo is the man that I saw with Talia in the atrium. We need to find him."

Fez rushed in holding big bags of sauce and a men's dress jacket. He dropped everything

in a heap by the door before bending over to catch his breath.

"I thought you could use something with pockets for the sauce," said Fez, looking up at Jessica. He picked up a black men's dress coat

and handed it to her. "This probably isn't your size, but it will help keep you warm."

Jessica graciously took the jacket. "Then I'm on board!" she said. The hem fell to her knees and the sleeves had to be rolled numerous times, but it did the trick.

"We need to find Prince Theo," Ellie told Fez. "He's the one I saw with Talia in the atrium reading the secret note."

They ventured to the gym, determined and warm. After looking around for several minutes, they couldn't spot Theo anywhere. *Where could he be?* Ellie wondered.

Just then the room went black, and the silhouette of a large monster appeared in the doorway.

Chapter Eight
The Lava Monster

POOF! Ellie fluttered under the table and Jessica dived after her. Ellie's heart sat in her throat as she saw what could only be described as a glowing lava monster inching closer to the tablecloth. Its hand reached for the white linen and flipped up the fabric to reveal the terrifying face of… Fez?

"Fez! What happened?" Jessica asked. "And why are you glowing?"

Fez looked down at the bright red glow coming from his pockets before focusing back on Jessica. "Someone or something turned off the lights, and you're glowing, too!"

Jessica looked down at her glowing pockets. Fez was right! She reached in and pulled out

a squishy bag of sauce from her jacket pocket. Sure enough, it was the spicy concoction that gave off the warm glow.

"Did you see who it was?" Jessica asked.

Fez shrugged. "Nope, I couldn't make out much." He pulled Jessica out from under the table.

POOF! Ellie appeared next to them.

"We need to find out who turned off the lights," insisted Jessica. "I bet they're behind this!"

Ellie and Fez agreed, and they headed toward the door. Ellie arrived first and gave the handle a big tug, but the metal door wouldn't budge.

"Don't be like Talia. Try pushing," suggested Jessica.

Ellie tried pushing, but it still wouldn't move. They all tried to push and pull, but the door was frozen shut. After five minutes of effort, the trio slunk to the floor.

"What now?" asked Ellie. Neither of the others had an answer.

The silence of the gym was soon filled with a loud crunching. The girls looked over to see Fez snacking on a plate of what looked like

chips topped with purple mashed potatoes. "Want some?" he asked.

Ellie and Jessica both shook their heads.

"You sure? It's extra delicious with the hot sauce." Fez squeezed out a thick dollop of red sauce onto a chip before shoving it in his mouth.

"That's it!" announced Ellie as she sprang to her feet. "Fez, I need some hot sauce."

Fez looked down longingly at the bag he'd planned to use on his chips before handing it to Ellie.

Quickly, Ellie opened a corner and dripped some of the sauce on the cracks of the door. It hissed and sizzled until the door crackled free of the frost's icy clutch. Once in the hallway there was light, but no sign of anyone.

"Where do you think the monster went?" asked Ellie.

"Maybe it went— WOAH!" Suddenly Fez crashed to the ground.

"Are you okay?" Jessica and Ellie asked in unison.

Fez rubbed his elbow. "Yeah, I just slipped on this ice."

Ellie looked down at the stream of ice that trailed all the way from the gym down the hall. "If we find where this ice trail goes, I bet we'll find the monster. Fez, Jessica, let's follow that trail!"

Chapter Nine
Chunky Mummy

They tracked the ice trail all the way to the maintenance room in the basement. Ellie pressed her ear to the door, and sure enough, heavy breathing and monsterly sounds came from inside.

Ellie gulped. "Maybe we should wait until they come out. It's probably just Prince Theo behind this anyway. Right?"

"It looked more like a monster to me," said Fez.

"Some vampires can transform into creatures, so maybe Theo is one. Whoever it is, we need to get them to tell us how to fix this," Jessica said.

Jessica pointed to her watch. "We're running out of time. We need to do this now. Ready? On the count of three. One, two, three." On three, they flung open the door, catching a chunky-looking mummy by surprise. The mummy sprang from the dark corner and tried to dash away, but the team tackled him to the ground.

Ellie pulled her special monster spray from her pocket and gave him a good spritz. "Ha, we got you now, Mr. Monster!" Ellie roared.

The cushy mummy rolled around the floor and grumbled in monster language. That is, until he suddenly spoke perfect English. "Wait, guys. WAIT!" pleaded the mysterious fiend. "I'm Tink. My foster mom is the wedding planner, Shayla Jeffords. I was just trying to help her out when everything went terribly wrong. Please don't spray me again with..." Tink let out a couple coughs. "Is that lavender spray?"

Ellie's face grew hot. "No! It's not lavender spray… It's lavender *monster* spray."

Tink stuck out his tongue in disgust. "Well, either way, it tastes terrible," he replied.

Ellie beamed. "Good, then it works!"

Tink unpeeled a few of the layers of the clothing that engulfed him.

"What are you wearing?" Jessica asked.

"I grabbed some stuff from the lost and found," Tink said as he struggled to pull a sweater over his head. "I needed something to stay warm after I accidentally supercharged the air conditioning system."

"Supercharged the air conditioner? How?" Fez asked.

"And why?" Ellie added.

Tink sighed. "I was just trying to help Ms. Jeffords cool down the wedding. Now everyone is frozen and I can't figure out how to fix it. I supercharged the air conditioner using this special device I invented, but it worked too well." Tink pointed to what looked like a contraption made with a garbage can, vacuum cleaner, and an ice sculpture. "I tried to thaw everything by

turning on the heat. I even turned off all the lights around the building to get more power, but it still isn't warm enough."

"That ice trail must be where you dragged the ice sculpture," concluded Ellie.

"And that's why you turned the lights out on us," added Fez.

"Oops, sorry," mumbled Tink. "I didn't know there was anyone not frozen." Tink looked at the unfrozen trio. "Um, why aren't you guys frozen? I thought everywhere in the school froze, except here since there are no vents."

"Ellie and I were in the atrium," Jessica answered. "There aren't any vents in there, either."

Tink squinted at the blueprint of the school that sat on the table. "Oh, you're right!" Tink then looked at Fez. "Why didn't *you* freeze?"

"I had this," said Fez. He took a bag of hot sauce out of his pocket and plopped it on the desk.

Tink looked down at the red bag with raised eyebrows. "Because you have spaghetti sauce?" he asked.

"It's hot sauce," explained Ellie. "And it has super-heating powers. When you turned off the lights and closed the door, the door froze shut, but this stuff unfroze it."

A wide grin stretched across Tink's face. "How much sauce do you guys have?"

"I have a few bags here," replied Fez, "and there's a big pot of it in the kitchen. Plus, there are a few extra-large bags I hid in the kitchen vent for a snack later, but your supercharged air conditioning blew them too far down to reach."

"If you guys can get me that pot, I can supercharge the heating system and thaw everything. I know you guys don't know me, but—"

"We're here to help!" Ellie declared.

"We don't want to see the royal wedding ruined anymore than you do," Jessica assured.

"What they said," Fez chimed in.

Tears glazed Tink's eyes. "Thanks, guys."

The team quickly introduced themselves and drew up a plan. Tink reached inside his backpack, which seemed to have everything from gadgets to gum. He handed out walkie talkies to Ellie, Jessica, and Fez.

They knew what they had to do.

Chapter Ten
We Have a Problem

An icy blast of air sent a shiver through Ellie as she pushed open the girls' changing room. "Hello? Helloooooo?" Ellie called, but no one answered. As she rounded the corner, she found the soon-to-be princess, Ayanna, and all her bridesmaids still frozen. While everyone else in the building seemed to be slowly thawing, this bunch looked as if they hadn't started to melt at all.

Ellie crept closer to Ayanna. Even frozen, she was more beautiful than Ellie had imagined with her smooth, dark skin and voluminous curls—both still radiant even while covered in a thick layer of ice. Another shiver

surged down Ellie's spine. Why was it still so cold in here?

She walked around the room searching for the vent, but all she found were ice sculptures and flowers masking the plain brick walls of the changing room. Ellie pulled out her walkie talkie. "Umm, guys. We have a problem. The princess' dressing room isn't getting any heat, and I can't find a vent anywhere."

Tink's voice sounded on the radio. "The blueprints say that there should be a vent in the opposite corner to the door."

"Okay, I'll check," said Ellie. A large, heart-shaped ice sculpture sat in the spot that Tink had described. Upon closer inspection, Ellie noticed a vent, but not only was the sculpture completely blocking any air flow, it had fused itself to the metal cover. Ellie leaned into the ice sculpture, her feet slipping as she pushed with all her might.

"Did you find it?" asked Tink over the radio.

"I did, but there is an ice sculpture blocking it and it won't move!" Ellie answered.

"You're going to have to melt it, Ellie."

Ellie reached into her pocket and palmed the small bag of sauce. Not nearly enough to get through that huge block. "I don't have enough sauce," she replied.

"Well, you know where there is more…" Fez chimed in.

"No way! NO WAY!" Ellie cried. "I am not crawling into a vent to get those extra bags. There are spiders and bugs in there."

"Ellie!" Jessica called. "This could be the difference between saving the wedding or not. I'm busy setting up the atrium, Tink is dealing with the vents, and Fez is in the kitchen. You have to do it."

"I can't do it!" Ellie sulked.

"Think of your parents and what might happen if Theo takes the crown," begged Jessica. "What if he makes all vampire and human marriages illegal and they're forced to separate?"

Ellie's nostrils flared. She wasn't going to let that happen. She looked over at Ayanna and

pulled the walkie talkie back up to her mouth. "Fine! I'll do it."

"I'll make sure the air is turned off in that part of the school," Tink exclaimed.

Ellie stuffed the device into her coat pocket as cheers of encouragement from the others rang through the monitor. She rushed out the door and rounded the corner to the nearest vent. Squatting down, she carefully popped off the vent cover. With a quick stretch to the left and then to the right, *POOF!* She shrank into a bat and flapped through the metal shaft. Cobwebs coated her wings and the distinct smell of bugs filled her nostrils.

"Ew! Ew! Ew!" shrieked Ellie.

She flapped on and saw a glow farther down the tunnel. The sauce! Ellie's eyesight admittedly wasn't great when she became a bat, but was that a small, glowing bag scurrying towards her? A plump spider that clearly enjoyed the sauce scuttled down the vent, bringing Ellie to a screeching halt—literally. She

yelled at the top of her lungs, so much so that when she went to take a breath, she inhaled the spider!

Chapter Eleven
Vampire Popsicles

Cough! Cough! Crunch! Ellie accidentally bit down on the squishy creature and was greeted with a burst of flavor. A flavor both sweet and spicy, no doubt thanks to Fez's father's secret hot sauce. That spider was delicious!

Ellie's fear subsided. Could she really be afraid of something so tasty? She continued to cruise through the vent, lapping up every insect she could find. Even the ones that weren't stuffed with the sauce were a crunchy delight. Soon she found the real bags of sauce and grabbed two with her feet before flapping out the nearest vent.

POOF! "I've got the sauce!" she called into the walkie talkie. She raced into the dressing

64

room and poured the sauce on the statue. The ice sizzled and hissed—melting down into nothing but a puddle—and hot air poured in through the vent.

Ellie looked at frozen Ayanna on the other side of the room and then at her watch. *6:50.* Only ten minutes left for the wedding to

happen, and Ayanna wasn't going to thaw in time. Ellie squished the last big bag of sauce in her hand. She knew what she had to do.

With one big splat, the whole bag of red sauce coated Ayanna's icy exterior, and with a couple sizzles and crackles, she was free.

"What happened?" Ayanna cried. She looked over at her frozen bridesmaids and gasped. "Why are they vampire popsicles?!"

Ellie giggled. "I'll explain later! You need to go get married!" Ellie grabbed the princess' hand and rushed her to the atrium. The last of the chairs were being set up, and the sun started to set. It was still humid and muggy in there, but no one seemed to mind.

Prince Bennett arrived seconds later. "Ayanna! Are you okay?" he asked, his eyes trailing down to Ayanna's once-white gown, now splattered in red. "What's on your dress?"

Ayanna looked down, noticing the splash of color on her dress for the first time. "Umm, I'm not sure."

"It's sauce," Ellie chimed in. "It actually goes really well with spiders!"

66

The couple stared at Ellie blankly, but before either of them could ask any more questions, a man ushered them to the altar.

"There you are!" cried a familiar voice. Ellie turned to see her parents rushing toward her.

"Mom! Dad!" Ellie cried as she ran over to give them a hug.

Mrs. Spark reached down to a splotch on Ellie's shoulder, worry lines crinkled her still-perfect makeup. "Are you bleeding? Did you get hurt?"

Ellie looked over at the spot and laughed. "No, Mom. I'm fine."

Dad swabbed the sauce with his finger, rubbing it between his index and his thumb. "Just as I suspected, not blood." He licked his finger. "Wow! That is super spicy." Mr. Spark's face turned red as he let out a couple coughs.

"Will everyone please have a seat?" said a tall man beside the royal couple. "We need to start this wedding."

Chapter Twelve
The Invisible Message

After a quick wedding and a whole lot of explaining, Ellie took a seat at a reception table with her oldest friend, her two newest friends, and Prince Bennett.

"I just wanted to thank you all for saving the wedding," Bennett said. "I don't want to think about what would have happened without your quick thinking. Enjoy the reception, and let me know if you ever need anything." Before he walked away, the folded piece of paper that stuck out of Ellie's shoe caught his eye. "Are those my vows?" he asked.

Ellie pulled the paper out of her shoe. "I don't think so. I found this blank piece of paper in the atrium. I think it has invisible ink."

Prince Bennett smiled and pulled the flash-light-like device out of his pocket. "You are quite the detective, Ellie Spark." He shone the colored light on the paper to reveal a mess of handwriting.

"But why did your brother have it?" asked Ellie.

Bennett shrugged. "Probably his way of trying to stop the wedding. I also found him earlier in the library with this," he wiggled the small light, "so I'm not surprised." Ellie handed the vows over, and the prince went on his way.

"Hey Ellie, I have a question," said Fez in a hushed voice.

"Okay," said Ellie.

"What's it like to be able to turn into a bat?"

Ellie shuffled uncomfortably in her seat. She had been so caught up in the investigation that she didn't even realize that Fez wasn't a vampire. All her friends had always been just like her, and even though she interacted with plenty of humans at school and in town, she had never spent this much time with one. "It's

pretty cool," she answered, "except I can't control it all the time. Like when I get scared, it just kind of happens… that's why some people call me Scaredy Bat."

"I think it's super cool!" reassured Fez. "Before we moved here, we lived in a town that didn't allow vampires, so I don't know much about them."

"Can I ask you a question?" asked Ellie.

Fez nodded.

"Are you afraid of me at all because I'm a vampire?"

Fez paused for a moment before answering, "Nah, my parents have made friends with plenty of vampires since we moved here. But they never let me ask them questions and I have soooo many."

"Well, I'd be glad to answer some," Ellie said.

Tink popped his head into the conversation. "I have a question. Do you actually drink blood? All the textbooks say you do, but I just can't imagine."

"Oh, that's a good one! If you do drink blood, is it human blood?" asked Fez.

"And if so, where do you get it?" added Tink as he lifted his collar to hide his exposed neck.

Ellie began to sweat. She had never been asked so many questions about being a vampire before, or any for that matter, so she wasn't sure where to start.

Fez and Tink eagerly waited for Ellie's answer, but they were only met with silence.

Jessica giggled. "Guys, I think you're overwhelming her. It's true, ancient vampires used to go around biting necks and sucking blood."

Both boys lost all color in their faces as their skin flushed a ghostly white.

"But we don't do that anymore. That's so out of fashion," Jessica explained. "Now we pretty much eat whatever we want, although many of us still eat mostly meat. But stuff like humans would, like steak and chicken."

"And we are really drawn to red food." Ellie added, finally finding her words. "My Dad says it's because our brains associate the color with

meal time. I love red licorice! But black licorice is super gross." She scrunched her nose as she pictured the black candy.

Tink and Fez let out sighs of relief. "Well, blood drinkers or not, I think you guys are all awesome!" exclaimed Tink. "Thank you so much for helping me today. You're great detectives." He paused for a moment before adding, "I wish I could solve mysteries like you guys."

"You can!" exclaimed Ellie without missing a beat.

Tink looked down at the ground. "But what help can I be? I almost ruined today. You guys are the ones that saved the wedding."

"We couldn't have done it without your quick thinking to put the sauce in your machine," Jessica said. "Anything we did to thaw the wedding would have made it too late!"

Tink smiled slightly. "Well, I wouldn't have been able to do it without Fez's hot sauce. That stuff packs quite the punch."

"I just thought it was delicious. Ellie is the one who discovered it could melt things," said Fez.

"And I would have never had the courage to get the rest of the sauce to save Ayanna without Jessica," explained Ellie. She looked across the table at her three smiling friends and Ellie couldn't help but smile, too. "I think we make a pretty great team!"

Chapter Thirteen
Detectives and Heroes

*R*ight before the clock struck seven, Ayanna and Prince Bennett were married. If the ceremony had taken place mere moments later, the prince would have had to renounce his crown, but this story has a happy ending. The Royal Vampire Wedding was saved, all thanks to these four middle school kids: Tink Taylor, Jessica Perry, Fez Fitzgerald, and Ellie Spark. If you ask us, our small town has quite the group of detectives and heroes on our hands!" said the reporter.

The four detectives proudly beamed and waved at the camera.

"This is Kelly Anders for Channel 5 News. Back to you, Karl."

Ellie flicked off the TV and smiled at her sister.

76

Penny's mouth sat wide open as she stared at the now-blank TV. "I can't believe that you saved the day. You're a big Scaredy Bat."

"Well, maybe I'm not anymore."

Penny laughed. "Yeah, right! You are too."

Ellie shrugged and yawned. "Anyway, I've

had a big day, so I'm going to bed." She headed upstairs and pulled back the sheets in her coffin, revealing a surprise bedmate.

As the hairy, eight legs inched their way towards Ellie, Penny smirked in the doorway. "What are you going to do, Scaredy Bat?"

Ellie picked up the spider by one of its legs, opened her mouth, and plopped it right onto her tongue.

Penny's eyes widened, and her face turned a sickly green.

Ellie swallowed and licked her lips. "Delicious!"

Penny raced the other way. "Mom! MOM!" she cried.

Ellie giggled. Maybe she *wasn't* a Scaredy Bat anymore.

Just then a crack of thunder shook the house, and *POOF!* Ellie flew under her bed.

Okay, so maybe she was still a *little* bit of a Scaredy Bat. But Scaredy Bats make the best detectives.

Hi!

Did you enjoy the mystery?

I know I did!

If you want to join the team as we solve more mysteries, then leave a review!

Otherwise, we won't know if you're up for the next mystery. And when we go to solve it, you may never get to hear about it!

You can **leave a review** on Amazon, Goodreads, or wherever else you found the book.

The gang and I are excited to see you in the next mystery adventure!

Fingers crossed there's nothing scary in that one...

The mysterious adventures of Ellie Spark in

Scaredy Bat

  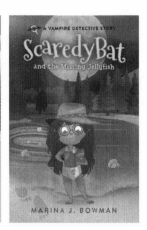

Also by Marina J. Bowman:
The Legend of Pineapple Cove

To learn more, visit marinajbowman.com

Don't miss
Book #2 in the series

Scaredy Bat and the Sunscreen Snatcher

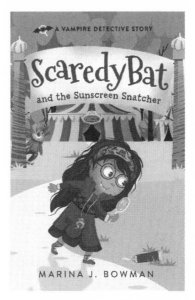

She's a clever young vampire. But she's terrified of everything. Can she summon some courage, or will the Garlic Festival be her doom?

Order Now!
scaredybat.com/book1next

Are You Afraid of Spiders?

Arachnophobia is the extreme or irrational fear of spiders and other eight-legged arachnids (like scorpions). Arachnophobia comes from the Greek word for spider, which is "arachne," and "phobos," the Greek word for fear.

Fear Rating: Arachnophobia is one of the top 10 most common phobias in the world. People with this phobia usually get panic attacks, faint, sweat excessively, cry, or scream at the sight of spiders.

Origin: Fear of spiders is an evolutionary response, and developed from the association between spiders and diseases in the past.

- Most spiders are not harmful to humans. They only bite in self-defense, and have no more effect than a mosquito bite.
- Only 2 kinds of spiders in the U.S. are venomous to people: the black widow and brown recluse.
- In the world, only 25 species of spiders can harm humans, out of about 40,000.
- Spiders eat over 2,000 insects a year, preventing our homes and gardens from being overrun with flies and mosquitoes.
- Some cultures, such as native Americans, believe that spiders bring good luck and are seen as a symbol of wisdom.
- Fried spiders are a crunchy treat in some places, including Cambodia. DO NOT eat spiders without parent supervision!

Fear No More! Spiders do more good than harm. But if you believe you suffer from arach-nophobia and want help, talk to your parents or doctor about treatment options. For more fear facts, visit: scaredybat.com/book1bonus.

Suspect List

Fill in the suspects as you read, and don't worry if they're different from Ellie's suspects. When you think you've solved the mystery, fill out the "who did it" section on the next page!

Name: Write the name of your suspect

Motive: Write the reason why your suspect might have committed the crime

Access: Write the time and place you think it could have happened

How: Write the way they could have done it

Clues: Write any observations that may support the motive, access, or how

Suspect 1

Draw below

Name:	
Motive:	
Access:	
How:	
Clues:	

Suspect 2

Draw below

Name:	
Motive:	
Access:	
How:	
Clues:	

Suspect 3

Draw below

Name:	
Motive:	
Access:	
How:	
Clues:	

Suspect 4

Draw below

Name:	
Motive:	
Access:	
How:	
Clues:	

Who Did It?

Now that you've identified all of your suspects, it's time to use deductive reasoning to figure out who actually committed the crime! Remember, the suspect must have a strong desire to commit the crime (or cause the accident) and the ability to do so.

For more detective fun, visit:
scaredybat.com/book1bonus

Name:	
Motive:	
Access:	
How:	
Clues:	

Hidden Details
Observation Sheet
-- Level One --

1. What did Ellie find hidden under her sister Penny's bed?

2. What kind of animal does Ellie turn into?

3. Where did Ellie find her necklace at the beginning of the book?

4. What is Ellie's favorite snack?

5. What does Ellie always keep in the pocket of her detective coat?

6. Where did the royal vampire wedding take place?

7. Where were Ellie and Jessica when everyone else froze?

8. What did Fez have that prevented him from freezing?

9. What kind of monster appeared in the doorway when the lights went out?

10. Why didn't Tink freeze?

Hidden Details
Observation Sheet
-- Level Two --

1. What kind of necklace does Ellie wear?

2. What is the name of Penny's favorite stuffed bear?

3. What is the name of Ellie's school?

4. Who did Ellie see talking in the atrium when she first arrived at the wedding?

5. What was Fez eating when he first met Ellie and Jessica?

6. What did Ellie find that made her think the Jotun Frost Giants did it?

7. What was Talia holding in her frozen hand?

8. By what time did Prince Bennett and Ayanna need to be married?

9. What scent is Ellie's monster spray?

10. What was written on the paper Ellie found with invisible ink?

Hidden Details
Observation Sheet
-- Level Three --

1. Who is Penny's favorite celebrity?

2. What was the minimum age to attend the royal vampire wedding?

3. Why did Ellie's family get invited to the wedding?

4. What sits on the shelf above the TV in Ellie's house?

5. Where does Ellie's grandfather appear in the story? (hint: he has a mustache and detective hat)

6. Who is Shayla Jeffords?

7. What does Jessica's mom do for work?

8. What is the name of Fez's family's restaurant?

9. What kind of ice sculpture was blocking the vent in the girls dressing room?

10. Who does Ellie have a poster of in her room?

For more detective fun, visit:
scaredybat.com/book1bonus

Level One Answers

1. A spider
2. A bat
3. On Penny's stuffed bear
4. Blood pudding
5. Monster Spray
6. Ellie's school
7. The atrium
8. Hot sauce
9. Lava Monster aka Fez
10. No vents in the basement

Level Two Answers

1. Purple dragon necklace
2. Miss Batty
3. Trenton Academy
4. Talia and Theo
5. An ice cream cone
6. A gray ball of fluff
7. A black marker
8. Seven o'clock
9. Lavender
10. Prince Bennett's vows

Level Three Answers

1. Silvia Romez
2. Twelve
3. Her dad performed surgery on King Stanton
4. A crystal egg
5. A framed picture in the living room
6. Tink's foster mom and the wedding planner
7. Acting
8. Hudson Heat
9. A heart-shaped ice sculpture
10. Hailey Haddie

Answer Key

Discussion Questions

1. What did you enjoy about this book?

2. What are some of the major themes of this story?

3. Who was your favorite character? What did you like about him/her?

4. Is the setting important to the book? In what ways?

5. How are Ellie, Jessica, Fez, and Tink similar? How are they different? How did they help each other in the story?

6. If you could turn into a certain type of animal whenever you wanted, what kind of animal would you choose? Why?

7. What fears did the characters express in the book? When have you been afraid? How have you dealt with your fears?

8. What other books, shows, or movies does this story remind you of?

9. What do you think will happen in the next book in the series?

10. If you could talk to the author, what is one question you would ask her?

About the Author

Marina J. Bowman is a writer and explorer who travels the world searching for wildly fantastical stories to share with her readers. Ever since she was a child, she has been fascinated with uncovering long lost secrets and chasing the mythical, magical, and supernatural. For her current story, Marina is investigating a charming town in the northern US, where vampires and humans live in harmony.

Marina enjoys sailing, flying, and nearly all other forms of transportation. She never strays far from the ocean for long, as it brings her both inspiration and peace. She stays away from the spotlight to maintain privacy and ensure the more unpleasant secrets she uncovers don't catch up with her.

As a matter of survival, Marina nearly always communicates with the public through her representative, Devin Cowick. Ms. Cowick is an entrepreneur who shares Marina's passion for travel and creative storytelling and is the co-founder of Code Pineapple.

Marina's last name is pronounced baʊmən, and rhymes with "now then."

Made in the USA
Middletown, DE
30 May 2022